Angus Lost

TOLD AND PICTURED BY
MARJORIE FLACK

A Sunburst Book · Farrar, Straus and Giroux

When WINTER came Angus grew tired of the SAME YARD and the SAME HOUSE and the SAME CAT and all the SAME THINGS he knew all about.

Angus was curious about OTHER PLACES and OTHER THINGS such as— WHERE the MILK MAN came from and WHERE the WIDE ROAD went to and WHAT kind of animals CARS are and things like that.

So one day Angus slipped through the gate

and—

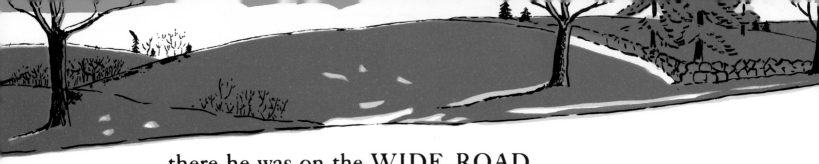

there he was on the WIDE ROAD.

Angus looked up the road and he could see no end.

Angus looked down the road and he could see no end.

Then ANOTHER DOG came by. "WOOOOF,"
said Angus.

"GRRRRUF," called the OTHER DOG.

So—

Angus and the OTHER DOG ran together up
the WIDE ROAD.

Faster ran the OTHER DOG, faster ran Angus,
but Angus's legs were TOO short.

Faster ran the OTHER DOG, faster ran Angus, but—
the OTHER DOG'S legs were TOO long.
Around the corner ran the OTHER DOG; around

the corner

ran Angus, but the OTHER DOG was GONE.
Instead there stood a STRANGER.

"WOOOOF," said Angus.

"BAA-AAAAA," said the goat.

"WOOOOF-WOOOOF," said Angus,

but

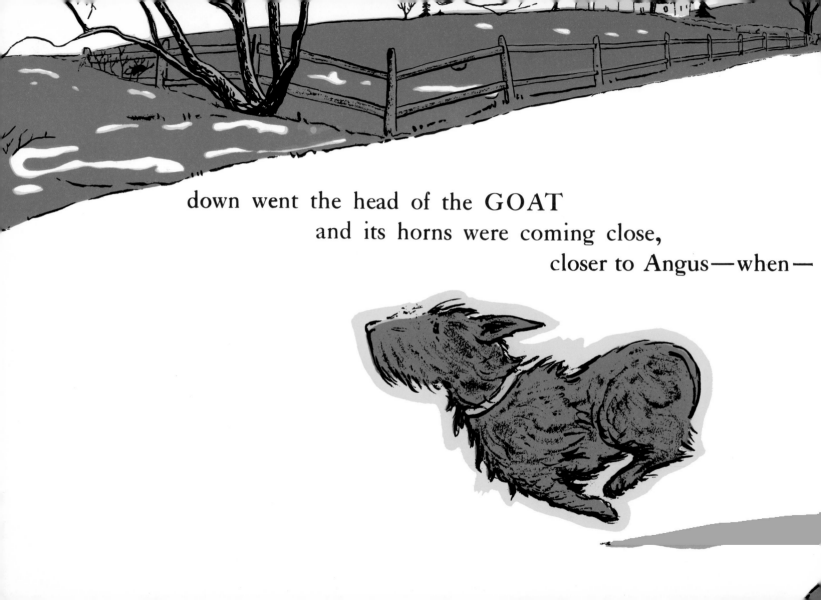

down went the head of the GOAT
and its horns were coming close,
closer to Angus—when—

the GOAT stopped, just in time!

But——ZOOOM

came a CAR, coming at Angus!

"WOOOOF," said Angus.
"HONK," said the CAR.
"WOOOOF," said Angus, and the CAR

ran away.

Then DARK began to come and Angus saw two EYES looking from a tree.

"WOOOOOOOF," said Angus and—

"WHOOO-WHOOO," called the EYES.
And Angus ran to find his house.

But

SNOW came, and
WIND came, and into a CAVE
crawled Angus, and he waited and

waited and waited until—

DAY came.

RATTLE-rattle-clink-clink—

there was the MILK MAN.

RATTLE-RATTLE-clink-clink-patter-patter.
Angus followed the MILK MAN

from door to door

from door to door until—

at last Angus was home again!
    Angus was glad to come back to the SAME YARD

and the SAME HOUSE and

the SAME CAT
and all the SAME THINGS
he knew all about.